"Power tends to corrupt,
and absolute power corrupts absolutely."
—Lord Acton, Historian (1834–1902)

ORDINARY BASIL

Island of the Volcano Monkeys

by WILEY MILLER

BLOOMSBURY

First published in Great Britain in 2008 by Bloomsbury Publishing Plc
36 Soho Square, London, W1D 3QY

Published by arrangement with Scholastic Inc.
557 Broadway, New York, NY 10012.

A CIP catalogue record of this book is available from the British Library

ISBN 978 0 7475 9473 4

All papers used by Bloomsbury Publishing are natural, recyclable products
made from wood grown in well-managed forests. The manufacturing processes
conform to the environmental regulations of the country of origin.

Printed in China by the South China Printing Company

1 3 5 7 9 10 8 6 4 2

www.bloomsbury.com

For Victoria, who makes

all things possible.

CHAPTER ONE

Missing

THE SPRING OF 1899 was a miserable time in the Pepperells' lighthouse. Twelve-year-old Basil was missing.

"How long has it been, ma'am?" the town constable asked as a light rain bounced off his cap.

"Two weeks, three days, and fourteen hours," replied Mrs Pepperell. Tears filled her red-rimmed eyes.

"I've seen this a hundred times, ma'am," the constable said. "Boys his age want more adventure. They think they're spreading their wings by running off on a schooner.

They always come home—knocked down a peg or two, and wiser for it in the long run."

"Always?" Mrs Pepperell seemed unconvinced.

"Well," the constable sheepishly replied, "most times."

"But it's not like Basil to do that," Mrs Pepperell said.

"Oh, I know what you're thinking. His mad great-uncle Arthur set off in a boat and never came back. But Basil's just an ordinary boy, not one given to running off like that."

"Had Basil been acting any differently lately?" The constable pulled out his notepad. "Or did he mention anything about meeting strangers?"

"Well . . ." Mrs Pepperell hesitated. "He talked about an adventure he had during the winter . . ."

"Ah!" the constable said excitedly. He began taking notes. "Tell me about it!"

"It was something about a man taking him off in a flying boat.

He said they went
to Helios, a city of
geniuses up in the
clouds. Then he
met a girl with a
giant flying reptile,
and . . ." Mrs
Pepperell stopped.
The constable
was smirking. He
put his pen away.

"It was just a dream, of
course," Mrs Pepperell said quickly.

"Hmm . . ." the constable muttered. "Well, I'd
better be getting back now." He tipped his cap and
then headed off in a small skiff. He heaved a sigh. It
didn't look good.

As Mrs Pepperell walked up the twisting staircase,
something in the lighthouse window caught her eye.
A small boat was rowing toward the island. "The
constable must have forgotten something." She hurried
back downstairs.

The boat pulled up to the dock, and a very tall, shadowy figure emerged. He carefully picked up a bundle and carried it to the front door. Then he gently put it down.

His long, thin fingers reached inside his drenched overcoat and pulled out an envelope. He placed it on the bundle before he returned to the boat.

As the man walked away, Mrs Pepperell opened the door. She didn't recognise the impossibly tall figure. "Who are you? What do you want?" she shouted through the din of pouring rain.

The man slowly turned. All Mrs Pepperell could see was a red eye peering out from the shadow of a broad hat.

"Just tell him zis," the man said in a thick Germanic accent. "Now ve are even." Then he disappeared into the darkness.

Mrs Pepperell looked down and pulled back the blanket covering the bundle on her doorstep.

"BASIL!" she screamed.

CHAPTER TWO

Monkey Island

A S THE SUN ROSE, a shaft of light lit Basil's
bedroom. In the chair next to his bed, Mrs
Pepperell sat beside her ailing boy.

Slowly Basil opened his eyes. "How . . . how did I get
back?" he asked.

"A tall man brought you home. I've never seen him
before, and I don't think I want to see him again. There
was something sinister about him—something . . . evil."

"Von Röttweil . . ." Basil sat up straight in both
surprise and fear.

"Do you know him?" his mother asked softly.

"Sort of," Basil said, trying to be truthful.

Then, reaching into a pocket of her dressing gown,
Mrs Pepperell pulled out an envelope, still damp from
the rain. "He left this note for you. He said you're even
now. What does that mean, dear?" She spoke as calmly
as she could, trying not to show her distress.

Basil opened the envelope and read the note. It was barely legible now that it was wet. *"'A . . . life for . . . a life . . .'"* He read haltingly, trying to make out the words. *"'The score . . . is tied . . . and the game continues.'*

"I have to get back." Basil threw off the quilt.

"Back where?"

"Monkey Island."

"Monkey Island? I've never heard of it. Are you sure it's not something you dreamed?"

"Oh, it's real, all right." Basil went on to tell his mother about the legendary volcanic island that sailors discovered in the most unlikely places. Some claimed to see Monkey Island in the North Atlantic, others said they saw it just a few miles off the coast of New England. But none of them could ever find it again.

"So if these top-notch sailors couldn't locate it," Basil continued, "how can an ordinary boy like me ever hope to go there a second time?"

"Well, you won't, dear," his mother said tartly. "You won't because you're going to stay right here—at home. How about a great big breakfast?" she added, changing the subject. "I'm going down to start cooking right now."

But Basil didn't want to go down to the kitchen. He had to get back to Monkey Island. But how? The lives of his friends depended on it!

His coat was next to the bed. He grabbed it and felt inside the pocket. "It's here!" His eyes lit up. He pulled out a flute—his friend Louise's flute.

Closing his eyes in concentration, he tried to remember what Louise had taught him. He pictured her showing him how to hold it, gently guiding his fingers over the holes to make the right pitch. "If you're ever in trouble," she had said, "hold it like this, and blow the note as long as you can. Don't worry if you can't hear it. The sound is still there."

Standing at the window, Basil tried. It was difficult, but he kept trying, over and over again. Each time, he blew until his lungs felt as if they would burst. Soon he was dizzy and had to lean on the windowsill.

Suddenly a familiar voice came through the window. "Ah, there you are, dear boy," the voice boomed. "I'd know that tune of yours anywhere!"

"Professor McGookin!" Basil looked up for the old man's flying ship, but the blue sky was empty.

"No, no," the professor said, laughing. "Down here this time!"

Basil's eyes widened in astonishment. The professor stood in a strange tube that popped out of the ocean.

"Come on, Laddie! We don't have much time!"

As the professor disappeared into the mysterious tube, a long ladder emerged and began to crank up to Basil's window.

Basil turned. He knew his mother would never let him go. The best he could do was leave a note. "I've gone back to Monkey Island," he wrote. "Don't worry. I'll be home in a day or so. I'll explain everything then." Carefully, he climbed out of his window and stepped down the ladder. He jumped into the professor's tube, and a heavy hatch door slammed shut behind him.

The professor sealed the hatch tight. Basil looked around. How could he not see a ship this big from his bedroom window? All he had seen was a metal tube. A large fish swam by. *Impossible.* "Are we underwater?"

"Yes," the professor said with a jovial smile Basil knew from his last adventure. "My newest invention! But first I need to know what's going on with you and Louise. Where is she?"

"She's on Monkey Island," Basil said and faltered. "And . . . and . . . she's in trouble."

The professor's grin disappeared, replaced by a worried frown. "Monkey Island? By herself?"

Basil tried to explain. "It started round couple of weeks ago. Louise came and asked if I wanted to fly to Monkey Island on Beatrice."

"Did she tell you she's forbidden to leave the city of
Helios? And that Monkey Island is not a place where
children are allowed? Not even adults can go there."

"Umm . . . I think she might have said something
like that," Basil muttered.

"But the two of you chose to go there anyway. Is
that right?"

"Yes, sir," Basil said, ashamed.

BASIL CLOSED his eyes, remembering that day, soaring high above the clouds on Beatrice, Louise's pet pteranodon. They had set out towards the north-east. After about an hour, Louise pointed down.

There, in the middle of the Atlantic Ocean, was an island! Not some rocky, barren outpost or an iceberg one might expect to see this far out, but a lush, green, tropical island with dense forests and coconut trees! And—most startling of all— an active volcano rose right out of the centre of the island, belching a plume of smoke and ash. *How can such a massive volcano be out here?* Basil wondered. Beatrice began her descent, and Louise turned to Basil. "We need to be very quiet! Whatever you do, don't talk to the monkeys."

Louise's tone was playful but sharp. Were they doing something dangerous? Basil knew Louise wasn't supposed to leave Helios, but she made the trip to Monkey Island sound like a harmless bit of fun. Now he wondered. What did she mean by "don't talk to the monkeys"?

As they came closer to the island, Louise guided Beatrice down to a beach on the north side. The air was filled with the sound of tropical birds, but Basil could also hear a faint, musical rhythm. It might have been the sound of the volcano, but the melody was strangely familiar. Could it be . . .?

Basil let the thought drop as they hopped off Beatrice, and Louise pointed to a path in the jungle. "Let's go!" she whispered.

They raced into a thicket of trees as Beatrice flew off to find something to eat.

The path took them to a steep staircase leading up the side of a massive wall. They rushed to the top. "Go on," Louise said. She pulled out a collapsible telescope. "Take a look!"

"I don't get it," Basil said. "Is this some kind of monkey village? I read that monkeys live in trees, not houses." Louise, as usual, was ahead of him and began to answer his questions even before he could ask them.

"Monkey Island," she explained, "is actually a giant, scientific laboratory. It was created by Von Röttweil, back when he was one of the leaders of the Helios High Council."

"The same Von Röttweil who almost killed us last January?" Basil asked in a horrified whisper. "What on earth are we doing here?"

"Don't worry," Louise said. "This island is completely hidden from Von Röttweil. He can't possibly find it. Listen, this is a fascinating place! That's why it's so off-limits, even to grown-ups. The monkeys here are clever—really clever. But nobody's supposed to get near them. As a matter of fact," she said with a mischievous smile, "we're not supposed to be here—*especially* without an adult."

"Then how did you get permission for us to come?"

Louise's silence said it all. She *hadn't* asked for permission, knowing full well she wouldn't get it.

Whoosh!

Louise put her hand on Basil's shoulder. "Shhh! Did you hear something? Listen!"

A rustling in the treetops below them began, then

stopped. It
began again, only
longer—and closer.

Wham! Something
orange shot through the
trees. Then a hook and a red
rope flew over the wall. *Zing!* A
monkey leaped up to where they stood.

He sat down and looked at Basil and Louise. Startled, Louise hissed, "You're not supposed to be up here!"

As the monkey's eyebrows dipped into a slight frown, he squinted, indicating disapproval. He slowly rose and looked them both in the eye.

"And neither are you," the monkey said.

Basil and Louise stood in stunned silence.

Then the monkey spoke again. "Why are you here? Which side are you on?" he demanded.

"My name is Louise, and this is my friend, Basil.

What's your name?" Louise struggled to speak in a lighthearted, chatty voice.

"Answer me!" the monkey snapped impatiently.

"We're just visiting for the afternoon. I don't know what you mean about being on a side." Louise twisted her hands nervously.

"It's simple," the monkey growled. "You're either with the resistance, or you're not."

"Resistance to what?" Basil asked, finally finding his voice. As he spoke, a shadow crossed over them.

When it did, the monkey shrieked, "A SENTINEL!" In terror, he scampered back down the wall, disappearing into the jungle below.

As the shadow passed, a sudden burst of air almost knocked Basil and Louise off the wall. But this wind had no sound. Scrambling to their knees, they looked up. Something was blocking the sun. Something enormous. "Is that Beatrice?" Basil asked, shielding his eyes.

"No." Louise's voice was shaking. "Bea always lets me know when she's coming."

"How can anything that big not make a sound?"

CHAPTER THREE

Owls

B ASIL'S QUESTION was answered when the creature soared further away. At a distance he could see it was an owl. But it was humungous.

Now Basil and Louise understood why the monkey was so frightened. Owls are hunters, and this owl was big enough to easily carry off a monkey. The majestic, silent hunter circled above. It was flying closer. *And it's big enough to carry off a meal that's even larger than a monkey,* Basil thought. *A meal like . . . us!*

The owl looked directly at the children and began to descend. They stood on top of the wall, frozen with terror as the great owl headed for them with its talons outstretched. Instinctively, Basil bolted. He was held back by Louise, who grabbed his coat.

"Wait!" she ordered.

"What?"

The giant owl was closing in faster.

"It can only focus on one target. If we split up too soon, it *will* catch one of us. On my signal, jump to your right!"

The owl was closer . . . closer . . . *closer*! Just as it was about to strike, Louise shouted, "NOW!"

Basil leaped to his right as far as he could, and Louise jumped to the left. The frustrated owl swooped between them.

Whoosh!

Again, a silent
gust of wind filled
the air. This time it was much stronger.
Both Basil and Louise were lifted off their feet. They
tumbled over the wall—where the monkey had gone!

As they plummeted towards the trees below, Basil grabbed the red rope. Helplessly he watched Louise crash through the rain forest canopy."LOUISE!" he wailed in a panic, hoping the thick foliage would break her fall. He dangled from the rope, listening for an answer. "LOUISE!" he howled again. "Can you hear me?"

The sound of snapping branches stopped.

"LOU-ISE!" Basil roared even louder.

Another sound came from below: *Crunch, crunch—* as if someone were walking on leaves. Then his blood ran cold. *Ooh-ooh-ahh-ahh-hee!* The distinct howls of excited monkeys.

"LOUISE!" Basil shrieked again through tears. His voice was cracking. "Are you all right?"

"She's alive," came a crisp voice from below. This time, when Basil looked down, the branches parted.

It was the monkey he'd seen before. "We'll keep her that way until we know what you're doing here." Then the monkey vanished.

What choice did Basil have? He shinned down the rope as fast as he could.

Don't lose sight of the monkeys and get lost in this jungle, he told himself. *Where am I? What is this weird place?* Then, behind a wall of bamboo, he spied a winding path. *This must lead to the monkeys,* he thought, *but which way should I go?*

Rustle. To his left, he caught a glimpse of a tail turning the corner. He followed it as fast as he could. The jungle path went on and on. Now Basil could see buildings. *Pant, pant.* He was ready to collapse.

Dense foliage and shadows made it difficult to see.
Crunch. He heard it again. *Uhhhhh.* Now it was a grunt.

Something is there. What can it be? A slight movement caught his eye. Two glowing eyes stared at Basil. The monkey!

The orange figure disappeared again. Basil ran.

Uhhhhh. That grunt again! When Basil stopped, he saw the same glowing eyes. But now a second pair of eyes pierced through the jungle greenery. Then another pair . . . and another. Soon the entire jungle was filled with eyes—all fixed on Basil. They surrounded him like a swarm of fireflies. Their leader silently stepped out of the foliage.

"Come," he ordered quietly. "Follow me."

Basil was trembling. "Where's Louise? Is she hurt?"

"I saved her life. Let her go!" he called up to a monkey in a tree.

Louise jumped down, shaking leaves from her hair. "It's true," she said. "But I'm covered with bruises. Oh, Basil, I'm—"

"Shhh! We need to hurry," the monkey said sharply, "before they find out you're here."

"They?" Basil and Louise said in unison. "Who are *they*?"

"I'll tell you when we get to the sanctuary."

CHAPTER FOUR

Professor McGookin

"HOLD THAT THOUGHT," Professor McGookin said, interrupting Basil's story to pull some levers and twist some knobs.

Basil didn't feel the ship turn, but the windows were moving. The sight made him queasy.

"What just happened?"

The professor grinned. "Good question, Laddie!" he boomed. "The inside of our ship is built on a musical gyroscope, which keeps it level no matter how much the ship turns. Otherwise, these books and charts would spill all over the floor."

"I see," Basil said, although he didn't really see at all.

"Now," the professor said, sitting down with Basil again. "Where were we?"

"Well, Louise and I followed the monkey back to a hidden cave. His name was Rathbone, and he was the leader of a secret resistance movement—a group

of monkeys who were trying to free the rest of the
monkeys from Lord Vex, the king of Monkey Island."

The professor was clearly distressed. "This is exactly

what we were worried about. Back when Von Röttweil was a trusted member of the High Council of Helios, he convinced us to let him do an experiment on monkeys. He invented a serum that altered their brain structure so they would become intelligent and live in peace. If

he could improve monkeys, he said we could improve humans. Then the civilisation of Helios wouldn't have to be hidden any more.

"Some of us resisted the idea. We argued that chemically changing nature could have catastrophic results."

"So how did it go wrong?"

"We didn't know anything *had* gone wrong," the professor replied. "The monkeys seemed to be living in peace. And when Von Röttweil was banished from Helios, he was banished from Monkey Island as well."

"So you left the monkeys alone, sir?"

"We did. But we kept the island away from the rest of the world, using the same ninth-dimensional musical power that hides Helios. We made sure Von Röttweil never returned there."

"But he found the island, sir, and . . . "

"Balderdash! That's impossible!" The professor's face reddened, but then he burst into a delighted smile. "You almost had me there, Laddie! Very amusing!"

"But Professor . . . "

Suddenly the professor pulled a tube from the ceiling. He beckoned to Basil. "Take a look."

Basil peered into the contraption.

He gasped. "Monkey Island!"

The professor returned to the control centre, and the submarine dived. Mesmerised, Basil stood at the ship's front window.

An immense, dark blur loomed ahead. *Zaroom!* As they came closer, Basil was shocked by what he saw. It was the *bottom* of Monkey Island! In fact, the island was not really an island at all. It was a colossal barge! Gigantic propellers and rudders kept it moving and steered it.

A vast metal tube extended below. They were heading straight for it.

"What *is* that?" Basil asked.

"It's a secret entrance," the professor replied. "It leads directly into . . . "

"The lagoon!" Basil cried.

"Yes!" the professor said with a start. "How did you know? Tell me the rest of what happened."

Basil took a moment to collect his thoughts. How could he describe everything that he had seen on Monkey Island?

CHAPTER FIVE

The Monkey King

O N THEIR WAY to Rathbone's secret sanctuary,
Basil and Louise had seen a peculiar structure in
the distance. It looked like a statue.

"That's the temple," Rathbone explained. "Stay as far
away from it as possible."

When Basil and Louise came closer, they recoiled in
horror. Could it be? Yes! It was a statue of Dr Von
Röttweil! It was a *temple* to Dr Von Röttweil! He was
being worshipped as a deity—a god!—by the monkeys.

"Most of the monkeys believe he created them," Rathbone explained, "and they obey his commands without question. Punishment is severe. The giant owls are his 'Angels of Vengeance', bred by Von Röttweil to patrol the outside wall. No monkeys can escape. Only the jungle hides us and keeps us safe."

"Von Röttweil may be a genius, but he's no god!" Louise snapped angrily.

"Yes, but it gets worse. We also have a Monkey King—Lord Vex. He claims to have been chosen by Von Röttweil. They rule under the strict doctrine of 'Peace Through Domination'. All of us are controlled by fear."

Basil and Louise knew plenty about Von Röttweil's plan for world domination. They had foiled that plan a few months earlier. Maybe Monkey Island was his Plan B—he would take over Helios with a trained army of monkeys. Then he would use the superior technology of Helios to take over the world.

But some, like Rathbone, *did* start to question him. Now they were determined to overthrow Von Röttweil, Lord Vex, and their army of Volcano Monkeys.

Rathbone led them into the sanctuary cave.

Crunch, crunch. He stopped. He signalled for everyone to be quiet. *Snap, snap.* Twigs were breaking. Footsteps slowly came closer. Now a large band of Volcano Monkeys stood at the entrance of the cave. They parted. The unmistakable figure of Lord Vex stepped forward.

All remained still in the cave. *Flash!* A beam of sunlight bounced off Lord Vex's crown. The rebels were exposed.

"Seize them!" the Monkey King bellowed.

The Volcano Monkeys rushed in. Darkness made
the fighting chaotic. Many rebels leaped out of the
cave, hoping to vanish into the safety of the trees. But
Lord Vex was prepared. *Crash!* The escaping rebels ran
straight into a net.

Louise and Basil were trapped in the rear of the
cave. Their only choice was to go deeper into the
unknown. Rathbone dashed alongside them.

Basil could hear the Volcano Monkeys close behind. It was pitch-black now. But when they turned a corner, a thin beam of light lit the back of the cave. An ancient door creaked open, revealing an elderly man in overalls. He was holding a wrench. A bushy white moustache covered most of his grizzled face.

"This way!" he rasped. "Hurry!"

Just as they rushed through the door—*wham!*—the elderly man slammed it shut. The door locked behind them. "You're safe now," he said.

Basil, Louise, and Rathbone followed the man down a rounded steel hallway. At the far end, a methodical rumbling filled the air. *Ka-thunk, ka-thunk, ka-thunk . . .* The closer they got, the louder the sound became. It was the unmistakable low rhythm of pistons from a steam engine. Alongside that sound, Basil could hear the higher whirring pitch of gears turning at different speeds. *Hisssssss.* Steam was escaping.

Emerging from the hallway, they found themselves at the centre of the volcano—which wasn't a volcano at all. It was an enormous engine room!

Straight ahead, a gigantic boiler belched out tremendous clouds of steam. Above it, a smokestack rose to the top of the room. Billowing clouds gave the illusion that this was an active volcano.

Looking down, Basil and Louise watched massive pistons churn while gears—the size of a house—turned the immense propellers under the island.

CHAPTER SIX

Volcano Vibrations

"RATHBONE, YOU'VE BEEN here before, haven't you?" Louise shook her head in wonder.

"Many times," Rathbone told her. He introduced them to the caretaker. They were old friends.

"I was once a loyal assistant to Dr Von Röttweil," the caretaker told them. "I worked in his laboratory in Helios. When I learned of his real ambitions, I was sickened by all of it. I left. I sailed home in a fishing boat, and I hoped I would never see Von Röttweil again."

"So how did you end up on Monkey Island?" Basil asked.

"I was marooned when my fishing boat was caught in a freak storm. It washed up on the shore of the island," the caretaker told them.

"My boat was powered by ninth-dimensional physics. Of course this island would act as a magnet . . . and my boat would never be able to travel far. So I've been here ever since, building this machinery and keeping it running."

"That's not all you've been doing," Louise said with a knowing smile.

"What do you mean?" asked Basil.

"The caretaker helped Rathbone start his resistance movement."

"How do you know that?"

"Can't you hear it? It's the music in the sound of the volcano. My mother calls it the 'ghost in the machine'. It's a very powerful sound. It runs the universe. Music. You *do* know that, don't you?"

Basil didn't want to appear stupid, so he simply nodded.

"The caretaker used the volcano to make musical vibrations that would help the most intelligent, educated monkeys like Rathbone to understand that Von Röttweil wasn't a god. You see?"

"I suppose so," Basil muttered. "It's that ninth-dimensional music again, isn't it?"

"Right, Basil. That humming sound in the volcano.

All active volcanoes have a musical vibration. I think it's absolutely *beautiful*."

"Anyway," Basil said, coming back to the problems ahead, "most of Rathbone's rebels were captured by Lord Vex and the Volcano Monkeys. We have to make a rescue plan."

"What will they do to the prisoners?" Louise asked.

The caretaker lowered his eyes.

"They'll take them to the the lagoon," Rathbone finally said with a groan of despair.

"What's the lagoon?" Basil asked.

"That's where Lord Vex takes nonbelievers for punishment," Rathbone explained. "The Angels of Vengeance do his dirty work."

"Well, how do we get them out?" Louise asked with her usual determination.

"It will take time," the caretaker said, "but time isn't on our side here."

"Then what are we waiting for?" Louise rolled her eyes in frustration.

"The sun is setting." Rathbone pointed. Through the opening of the volcano, they could see the moon rising.

"This is when the owls hunt," the caretaker told them. "No one goes out at night."

Patience was never Louise's strong point, but problem-solving was. "So," she said as she began to work out what to do, "night would be the perfect time to rescue the prisoners if we could find a way to keep the owls from hunting . . ."

"Very true," Rathbone said. "But how can we possibly stop the owls?"

"Well," Louise said, thinking aloud, "what keeps owls from flying?"

Basil had an answer. After all, he had spent a lot of time in the Maine woods. "Bad weather," he piped up. "But we can't control the weather."

Louise smiled brightly and winked at the caretaker. "No, we can't control the weather . . . " she said with the smile that drove Basil mad, a smile that meant she knew something he didn't.

" . . . but the island can!" the caretaker said, finishing off her thought.

Seeing the look of confusion on Basil's face, the caretaker explained that Monkey Island was able to hide from passing ships by creating its own fog bank. Piping the volcano's steam out to mix with the cool surface of the sea made a fog so thick it obscured the entire island.

"Will that be enough to keep the owls from flying?" Basil asked.

"No," the caretaker said, "but it will stop them long enough for you to set up rescue positions at the lagoon."

"What then? I thought we needed to have a storm big enough to keep the owls from flying."

"Well, we may not be able to create a storm, but we can steer the island into one!" With that, the caretaker climbed the metal steps to the master control panel—a dizzying wall of gauges, levers, and wheels that operated the engine and steered the island.

"How are you going to find a storm in time?" Basil pressed on, wanting to understand.

"We'll head to the North Atlantic," the caretaker yelled down as the racket of grinding gears and billowing steam became a roar. "There's never a shortage of storms there!"

CHAPTER SEVEN

Stormy Weather

"**B**RILLIANT!" THE PROFESSOR shouted, interrupting Basil's story with a beaming smile. "Climate control! Sooner or later, Louise always comes up with a solution to any problem facing her."

"Yes, it was a great plan—but it needed to be timed perfectly. We spent the next few days heading north in search of a storm big enough to keep the owls from flying.

"In the meantime," Basil continued, "the caretaker kept the island in a dense fog so we could go out undetected and survey the lagoon for the rescue."

THE LAGOON WAS a perfectly round body of water at the base of the temple. At its centre was a bottomless eddy—a rip tide that sucked everything into its abyss.

The rebel monkeys were held in a cage suspended directly over it. Escape was impossible.

When the caretaker and Louise finally found the storm they needed, everyone got into position under the cover of fog at dusk.

Their plan
had to take
place in the
dark when
the Volcano
Monkeys
were afraid
to be outside.

Meanwhile, the storm would keep the owls grounded.

That night, as soon as the storm hit, Rathbone climbed across the wire holding the cage. It was slippery from the rain, and the wind roared. Carefully he unlatched the door.

The rebels scattered into the jungle, and Basil, Louise, and Rathbone headed back to the volcano. Their plan had worked perfectly.

As they passed the temple, Basil noticed a light shining out from the bottom of the wall. Down below, in a room with iron bars on it, something moved!

"We have to go in there!" Basil yelled through the storm. "It might be more prisoners!"

"Over here!" Louise called. She pointed to a crack in the wall. Basil pushed, and a secret door slid open. Inside, winding stairs curved downwards.

Basil led the way, and as they descended, he heard a moan. "It's a man!" he cried. As Basil and Louise inched closer, the man's head turned out of the shadow and into the light. Basil and Louise pulled back in shock.

It was Dr Von Röttweil! And he was chained
to the wall in the
very temple
built to
worship
him!

"He's been drugged," Rathbone said with certainty.
"They used poison darts. The tips are rubbed on the
back of a Hallucifrog, coating them with a liquid that
puts you to sleep."

"How do you know that?" Louise asked.

"It's a weapon he gave us when I was in his army. We were told it was to defend our island, but he was really training us for an invasion. Ironic, isn't it?" Rathbone said. "He's been attacked with his own weapon."

Basil and Louise knew that Von Röttweil's first plan had been to build an army of robots. When that failed, Von Röttweil turned to Monkey Island.

"Lord Vex must have hidden Von Röttweil away so no one else would discover that he isn't a god—only a man," Rathbone said.

Von Röttweil was barely conscious, but he began to cough. "If I escape," he gurgled, "Vex vill murder me."

"In that case," Basil asked, "why didn't Lord Vex just do away with you before?"

"Because," Von Röttweil sputtered, "he vanted . . . to know everyzing about za island . . . and how it vorks . . ."

Von Röttweil paused, trying to clear his mind. "Ze experiment is a failure . . . and must be terminated . . ."

"Basil," Louise said softly, "once Lord Vex knows how the island operates, there won't be any need for Von Röttweil . . . or the caretaker!"

"We can't let Von Röttweil destroy the island!" Basil exclaimed. "He tried to *kill* everybody! I say we leave him to rot. Let's take our chances against Lord Vex and the Volcano Monkeys."

"No," Louise shot back. "As horrid as he is, Von Röttweil is more useful to us and to the resistance alive. It's the only way the rest of the monkeys will learn the truth—just as Rathbone has."

Basil couldn't argue with her logic. "OK. But how are we going to get him out of here?"

Louise reached for the ribbon around her waist and pulled out her flute. She gently touched the sound holes, producing a long, piercing note.

Soon the locks on Von Röttweil's chains began to shake. They snapped open.

Louise handed the flute to Basil. "Put this in your pocket for now, Basil. Hurry! I'll tie it on later. We have to get him out of here before Lord Vex captures us!"

They helped Von Röttweil to his feet and up the stairs. He was still confused and barely able to walk.

The storm had passed and fog was thickening again as they pushed through the jungle. Von Röttweil stumbled
and fell just as they approached the volcano entrance.

"Wait! I hear something." Rathbone held up his hand.

In the thick grey fog, a twig snapped. For just an instant, the mist cleared, and they could see ahead. A few metres away, Lord Vex and his Volcano Monkeys stood, poised to attack.

Gently, rain began to fall again, thinning the fog. The Volcano Monkeys, armed with blowguns, awaited the order from Lord Vex.

"You can come peacefully or very peacefully. It's your choice," Lord Vex snarled. "The power play is over." But what he and the Volcano Monkeys didn't see was Von Röttweil. He was finally waking up.

Von Röttweil raised his head. A little wobbly, he held on to a tree trunk to keep his balance. Slowly he stood to his full, seemingly impossible height.

The Volcano Monkeys dropped their weapons and bowed in fear and obedience.

With lightning speed, Lord Vex grabbed one of the blowguns. He wildly fired a poison dart at Von Röttweil and missed. The doctor staggered behind a tree for cover.

The Volcano Monkeys were completely confused. Their hesitation gave the rebels a quick chance to escape. "Run!" Rathbone shouted, leading them into the jungle.

"No!" Von Röttweil barked. "Zis vay!" He pointed in a different direction. "Ve must get off ze island!"

"See?" Lord Vex screeched. "Our almighty god wouldn't run away! He's an impostor—a fake!"

Grabbing their blowguns, the Volcano Monkeys ran, stopping only long enough to fire their darts.

As they tore through the thick jungle, Basil and
Louise could hear the *THOK-THOK-THOK* of poison darts
hitting the trees. Up ahead, the high wall blocked
their escape.

"How can we get to the other side?" Basil shrieked.
THOK-THOK-THOK!

"Follow me!" Von Röttweil called. By now he was fully awake. He yanked some giant leaves aside, revealing a hidden door. The hinges were rusted, and jungle vines had sealed it shut.

Rathbone ran at the door, leaping feetfirst, kicking with all his might. *THOK!* A dart whizzed by his head and stuck in the door. *Wham!* Rathbone kicked again and again. Finally the door burst open.

On the other side of the wall, a small rowing boat lay on the beach, upside down.

As they rushed through the door, more darts shot past them. *Slam!* Von Röttweil locked the door just ahead of another volley of darts.

THOK-THOK-THOK! How could they get to the rowing boat before the Volcano Monkeys climbed to the top of the wall?

Rathbone, by far the fastest, raced to the boat and flipped it over.

THOK-THOK-THOK! Darts began to hit the boat. The Volcano Monkeys were now on top of the wall and had a clear shot.

Basil, Louise, and Von Röttweil fled back to a ledge beneath the wall for safety. *Now what?*

Suddenly, the clouds parted. "Sunshine!" Basil cursed. "Another advantage for the monkeys. We'll never get away now!"

"AAAGGGHHRR!" A bloodcurdling yelp from the top of the wall shattered the silence. Then more screams . . . screams of absolute terror.

"What is it?" Louise scanned the beach. "Owls!" Huge shadows streaked across the white sand.

"Zis is our chance!" The doctor dashed towards the rowing boat with Basil and Louise close behind. For a moment, the owls focused on the monkeys.

Then they
turned their
attention to the beach.
Louise stopped in her
tracks. "Go, Basil! Keep running!"
Basil had learned to trust Louise
completely. He bolted for the rowing boat
while Louise ran back to the wall. Once there,
she reached for the ribbon around her waist.
No! Her flute was gone! It was in Basil's pocket!
Meanwhile, Basil and Rathbone made it to
the boat. Von Röttweil crouched beside them.

Peeking out from under the
boat, Basil watched Louise
cling to the wall. "Basil!"
she cried. "The flute!"

Basil pulled the bamboo
flute from his pocket. "What do you want
me to to do?"

"Play it! Play the first notes I taught you!"

Basil lifted the flute to his lips and blew. He
didn't hear anything, but he hoped that meant
he was doing it right.

"Again!" Louise shouted, and Basil blew harder.

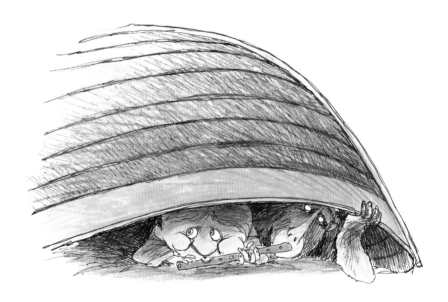

Just then, an ear-piercing screech filled the air. The
unmistakable shadow of Beatrice jetted across the sand.

The owls were no match for the flying pteranodon.
They scattered in fright. As the owls disappeared,
Louise ran out on the beach. "Bea! Down here!"

The mighty wings tucked in. But as Beatrice
swooped down, Louise heard a strange whistling.

Fump. It was followed by the sickening thud of a poison dart hitting flesh. Beatrice screeched in pain and anger. She spread her wings to protect Louise. *Fump!* She was hit again.

Fump . . . fump . . . fump . . . .

From under the rowing boat, Basil and Rathbone watched in horror as Louise cradled her magnificent pet. Beatrice slumped into an unconscious sleep from the drug.

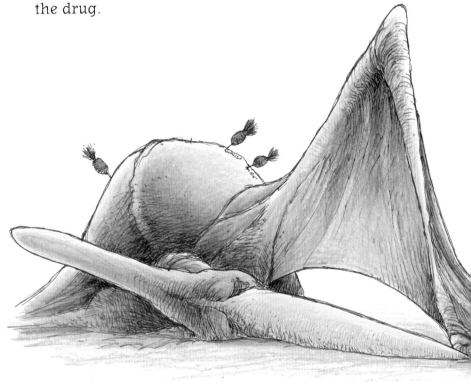

THOK-THOK-THOK-THOK-THOK! With Beatrice down, the monkeys returned, striking the wooden hull of the rowing boat with their poison darts.

"Wait here!" Rathbone ordered. He sprinted out, pulling Louise away from Beatrice. They ran to the boat, but *THOK-THOK-THOK . . . Fump . . . fump . . .*

Louise and Rathbone crumpled as the drug immediately took effect.

Quickly Von Röttweil scooped up Basil, lifted the
rowing boat, and dragged it behind them as a shield.

"No!" Basil protested. "We can't leave the others!" But
he was no match for the doctor.

THOK-THOK-THOK!

As soon as they reached the water, Von Röttweil
turned the rowing boat over and shoved Basil in. Poison
darts continued to whizz past them.

"Ve must get to za ship!" Von Röttweil began rowing
as hard as he could. "Zen ve'll be . . ."

THHH-UPP.

This time it was the sickening sound of a dart shooting past Basil's ear and striking Von Röttweil.

"You . . . must . . . row . . ." Von Röttweil managed to sputter before he slid into unconsciousness.

Basil looked back at the island. How could he leave Louise and Rathbone behind? *But Von Röttweil was heading for a ship. For help! I have to try!* He shoved the doctor aside. Then he began rowing with all his might, as if he were back in Maine. Soon the sound of whizzing darts disappeared, and the sea breeze freshened. Up ahead, Basil spotted a strange, metal ship. It must be Von Röttweil's!

He tied the rowing boat to the stern of the peculiar craft and climbed aboard. He'd grown up sailing and easily took the ship out to sea. He headed west, towards the setting sun. He would go home and get help.

As the sky darkened, storm clouds gathered ahead. He wouldn't be able to navigate by the stars—a skill handed down the generations in Basil's seafaring family. Alone, at sea, in the darkness, with Von Röttweil asleep in the rowing boat trailing behind, Basil was at a loss what to do. He reached in his pocket and pulled out Louise's flute. He blew.

Nothing happened.

He moved his fingers on the holes and tried to make up his own tune. Much to his surprise, moments later, lights went on and revealed an elaborate compass. Basil knew how to log in the coordinates of a specific longitude and latitude. In fact, he could probably steer the ship straight to Maine! The wind was picking up, and the sea grew choppy as he sailed the ship home, into the storm.

Waves rose higher and higher, rocking the ship and
the tiny rowing boat. Von Röttweil was nearly thrown
into the cold, unforgiving
sea, yet he
slept on.

Near complete exhaustion, Basil fought to keep the ship on course and to stay on board.

Flash! Through the wind and rain, something bright lit up the distance. A few seconds later, it flashed again. Basil blinked. The light began appearing in a precise rhythm. That could only mean one thing . . . a lighthouse! *I made it back home!*

As Basil let out a jubilant cry, the retaining line of the sail caught him in the ribs, knocking the wind out of him. He was hurtled into the turbulent water.

"Help!" he cried in the darkness, desperately trying to swim back to the ship. But he couldn't fight the power of the sea.

A beam of light flashed across him from the lighthouse. *What is it?* Something . . . somebody . . .

grabbed the back of his jacket. Lapsing in and out of consciousness, Basil felt himself coughing seawater out of his lungs. Dazed, he opened his eyes just long enough to glimpse the blurry image of Von Röttweil's face.

"A life for a life," he heard the doctor say. "I alvays repay my debts."

CHAPTER EIGHT

Home Sweet Home

BUBBLES ROSE in front of the submarine's window. A rumbling sound broke through Basil's reverie.

"And that's the last thing I remember before waking up in my bed," Basil said.

"Perhaps there's some hope for Von Röttweil yet," Professor McGookin replied with tentative optimism.

"I'm not so sure." Basil remained glum. "I think he plans to destroy Monkey Island . . ."

McGookin's submarine was now approaching the tube below the island.

"Hang on, Laddie! We're going in!" Faster and faster they spun. Then, with a *whoosh*, they broke the surface.

Basil looked out of the window in astonishment. They were floating in the middle of the lagoon!

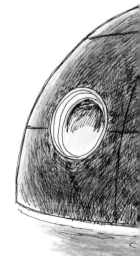

Professor McGookin opened the hatch.

The first thing Basil noticed was the quiet. The monkeys had disappeared! *What had happened?*

Von Röttweil's temple was now a small mountain of rubble. "Where is everyone?" Basil asked.

The professor pulled out a telescope. "Aha!" His face lit up in a smile. "There," he said, pointing at the secret entrance to the volcano. He handed the telescope to Basil.

"Professor!" he cried. "I can see Louise! What do you think is going on?" As he watched, dozens of monkeys went in and out of the entrance.

Slowly the submarine chugged to the shore. "There's only one way to find out." The professor opened the hatch door, and the ladder slowly unfolded.

Basil bolted to dry land, racing towards Louise and the others. A sudden shadow made him skid to a stop.

"Professor! The owls!" he cried and crouched behind a boulder. But the shadow was only a passing cloud. "Where are they?" he asked.

By now the professor had reached the boulder. "Come on, Laddie," he said in a jovial baritone. "Let's go and see."

CHAPTER NINE

Moving Shadows

THEY DIDN'T HAVE to go far to get answers. Their arrival was spotted, and running down the path was Rathbone. Louise raced past him and leaped into the professor's arms, laughing and crying at the same time.

Basil stood still, but he was grinning. Louise jumped over and hugged him, kissing him on the cheek. "See? I knew you could do it!"

Basil's face turned bright red. He had never been hugged by a girl before, much less kissed. The exception was his old aunt May—but that didn't count.

Louise, delighted by his discomfort, giggled and kissed him again. It was impossible for Basil to form a clear thought.

"All right, young lady," the professor bellowed with a hearty laugh, "I think our boy's had enough. Now tell us what happened."

"Perhaps we should start with introductions."
Rathbone came out from the jungle trail.

"Indeed," the professor said without a hint of
surprise.

"Excuse my manners," Louise said, finally letting go
of Basil. "Professor McGookin, I would like to introduce
you to our friend, Rathbone."

"A-hem . . ." The caretaker stepped forward and gave Louise that parental look that reminded her that she was forgetting something.

"Oh . . ." Louise said, slightly embarrassed. "Forgive me. I mean *President* Rathbone!"

"An honour to meet you, sir." The professor extended his hand.

"The honour is mine, Professor. I've heard a great deal about you. We have much to discuss."

As they headed back to the volcano, Basil turned to Louise. "Beatrice. What happened to Beatrice?"

An ear-piercing screech echoed down from the top of the volcano.

"She's fine. She's still pretty groggy from all the poison darts, but she'll be as good as new soon."

"So what happened here?"

"Well, when the Volcano Monkeys saw that Von Röttweil was just a man and not a god, most of them began to question Lord Vex. Only a few of them ran. Rathbone and his rebels are in control now. It's lovely, isn't it?"

"And Rathbone is president?"

"The monkeys all wanted Rathbone to be their new
king. But Rathbone's much cleverer than that. He
wanted the power to be shared. He formed a democracy.
All the monkeys vote now—about everything."

"They *are* intelligent, aren't they?" Basil said.

"Rathbone wants all the monkeys to learn the
secrets of how the island works. That way they can
literally steer their own destiny."

Louise and Basil reached the entrance to the engine room. It was full of monkeys, all learning about the island's machinery. The caretaker was supervising. Everything was going well.

The professor joined them at the entrance and looked out at the jungle. He frowned.

"What is wrong, Professor?" Louise asked.

"The shadows." Puzzled, McGookin walked outside and stood motionless in the sunlight. He looked down at his feet. "Watch my shadow," he instructed.

Basil and Louise watched in amazement. His shadow was slowly moving around in a clockwise direction.

"What does that mean?" Basil asked.

"It means . . . the island . . . is moving in a circle! ARTHUR!" The professor roared and rushed inside.

"Yes, Professor?" the caretaker shouted back, trying to be heard over the loud machinery.

"FULL POWER ASTERN!"

The caretaker didn't hesitate. The island jerked forward.

"Come quickly!" the professor ordered Basil and Louise. "Back to the submarine! We don't have much time!"

As Basil and Louise ran across the beach, the island began to tilt. They could barely keep their balance. Finally they climbed the ladder and leaped into the submarine. The professor slammed the hatch shut.

"Strap yourselves in, children," the professor directed. "We're going down fast."

The roar of a billion bubbles obscured their vision. At lightning speed, the submarine descended down the tube connecting the lagoon to the sea.

Once they were back in the open water of the

Atlantic, the blinding bubbles disappeared. At first
Basil and Louise didn't see anything but fish and
debris swirling past them. "What's *that*?" Basil asked.

"I don't know. I can't make it out," Louise said. But
as they got closer, their eyes widened.

"It . . . it . . . " Basil stammered, "it looks like a . . .
tornado!"

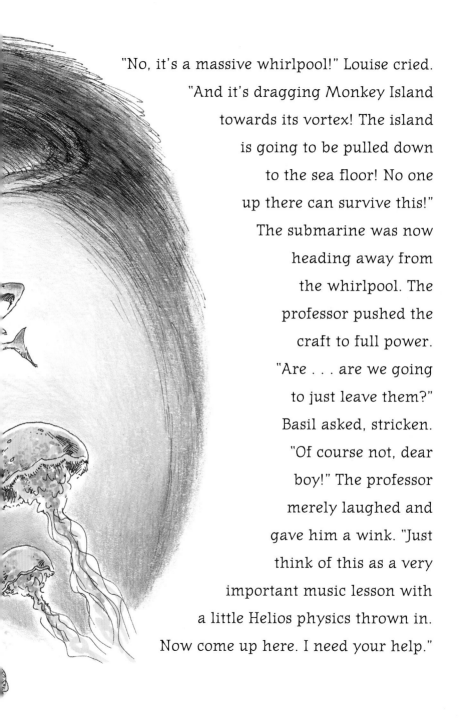

"No, it's a massive whirlpool!" Louise cried. "And it's dragging Monkey Island towards its vortex! The island is going to be pulled down to the sea floor! No one up there can survive this!" The submarine was now heading away from the whirlpool. The professor pushed the craft to full power. "Are . . . are we going to just leave them?" Basil asked, stricken. "Of course not, dear boy!" The professor merely laughed and gave him a wink. "Just think of this as a very important music lesson with a little Helios physics thrown in. Now come up here. I need your help."

Basil and Louise climbed to the control centre.

"Louise," the professor said sternly, "I want you to take the helm and keep the ship on course."

Louise grabbed the wheel. She solemnly nodded.

The professor pulled Basil to the starboard side of the helm. "When I give you the signal," the professor instructed, "pull this lever down fast—as *hard* as you can. Will you do that, dear boy?"

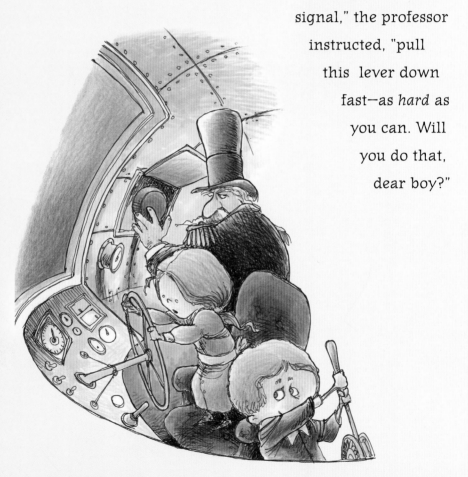

Basil grabbed the lever and nodded.

The professor then raced to the other side of the helm. "We'll be in position in a few seconds!" he called over the roar of the engines. "Hold steady, Louise! Basil, wait for my order!"

The professor pointed the bow of the ship straight up, then stopped the propellers. The bottom of the submarine faced the whirlpool in the distance.

"Ready, Basil?"

Basil gulped. "Ready, sir!"

"When I give the signal . . ." The professor lifted a small metal cover, exposing a large red button.

He took a deep breath and then slammed his hand on the button. "NOW!" the professor thundered.

A hatch opened on the bottom of the ship, exposing a cone-shaped device. The professor ramped the propellers up to full speed as Basil jerked the lever down with all his might.

A sonic wave of musical notes from the ninth dimension boomed from the cone-shaped device. It began rocking the ship, and the painful sound made Basil cover his ears. Then a rush of bubbles exploded as Basil's lever released the submarine's ballast water. With the propellers spinning at full speed, the craft rocketed towards the surface.

"HOLD STEADY, LOUISE!" the professor roared over the engines. The ship's hull rattled, straining to hold together under the staggering pressure. Faster and faster they shot upwards, finally exploding right out of the water, like a breaching whale. They crashed back down with a thundering splash.

Regaining their senses, Professor McGookin, Basil, and Louise found themselves safely aboard the ship, now bobbing gently in the water. It all seemed so calm.

"How . . . how did you do that?" Basil asked.

The professor was back at the helm, spinning the wheel rapidly. "It's not over yet," he responded. "I want both of you to get into your seats right now."

The ship was moving again, but it felt different— and Basil could hear the rhythm of a tune he had heard before but couldn't quite remember. He and Louise gave each other an identical quizzical look. "What's going on?" Basil asked.

"I don't know, but look at that." Louise pointed at the large window in front of them. The sea had been replaced by blue sky and some clouds.

Then a seagull flew past the window.

"What on earth . . . ?"

"Come on. Let's get a better look," Louise said. What they saw beyond the console left them speechless. The sea was a hundred feet below them! They were riding on the crest of a massive wave, and they were heading directly for the whirlpool!

In the distance, Monkey Island still skidded
on the outer edges of the swirling water,
continuing to spin towards the deadly vortex.
At the same time, far off in the distance,
something metallic reflected the sunlight.
Whoosh! The wave was now speeding faster
and faster as it raced towards the whirlpool.
"Hang on, children!" the professor cried.
As the giant wave hit the edge of the
whirlpool, it rose higher . . . and higher
. . . and higher. Soon Basil and Louise were
directly above the centre of the swirling sea,
looking straight down at the deep, dark hole.

"It's that sound again," Basil began, but he was silenced by what followed. The power of the spinning water sent the tidal wave crashing right down into the void. In seconds, a million gallons of water poured into the whirlpool, bringing its energy to an immediate stop.

As the wave came crashing down, McGookin's ship slid over the pounding surf and shot directly at Monkey Island. Slowing to a halt, the island bobbed in the last of the rolling waves.

Professor McGookin's shoulders slumped in relief. He turned to Basil and Louise and gave them his wonderfully reassuring smile.

"You did it, Professor! You did it!" The children leaped with joy.

"No," he answered quickly. "We did it. Now let's go to this island of yours and see if anyone is injured."

Once again, the professor took his ship underwater and headed for the tube that led to the lagoon. When they stepped on to dry land, they were met with celebration. The monkeys had all survived unharmed, and Lord Vex's followers had surrendered.

Back in the volcano's engine room, the caretaker was drenched with sweat. "Well done, old friend," the caretaker said softly. "Well done."

"Nothing you wouldn't have done, Arthur." The professor chuckled.

"Even with all our scientific knowledge, it's amazing how little we know, isn't it? Thank goodness for the power of music in the universe, eh?" Then, being a humble man, the professor abruptly changed the subject. "It appears we have some work ahead of us to get this island moving again."

"We do." The caretaker looked over at Basil and Louise, who were helping Rathbone repair a broken gear, using Louise's flute. "First you have to get these two home."

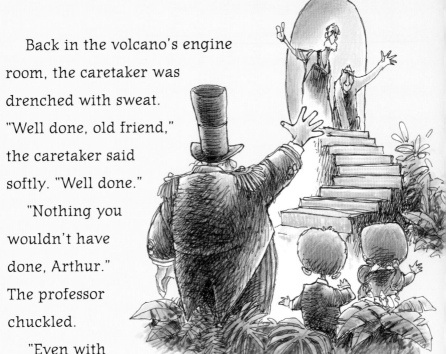

"Louise could help you. I know her mother would agree. She's quite brilliant at mathematics. She cracked a tenth-dimensional code when she was *six*, Arthur. Imagine! Think of what she could do on this island . . ."

The caretaker pointed to all the monkeys who were hard at work. "They have to learn to do this themselves. Besides, Louise is needed in Helios. The Council needs her. We all do."

With that, the professor sighed. "I suppose you're right. Besides, I'd miss her. It's nice to see her finally have a friend who understands her, isn't it?"

"Splendid. He's not from Helios, but he could have been. I can hear it in his voice."

"Oh, yes. He's the one we've been looking for. The connection, you know. Between his world and ours. But he doesn't see it yet."

"Does she?"

"Perhaps. She usually knows much more than I suspect, Arthur. After all, she came to Monkey Island just in time, didn't she?"

The professor turned to Basil and Louise. "Say your farewells now, children. It's time to leave."

Louise hugged Rathbone. "Are you going to be all right? Can you deal with Lord Vex? And . . ."

"Shhh." Rathbone held Louise's hands. "First of all, he's not Lord Vex any more. He's just an ordinary criminal. We'll be fine."

Rathbone then extended his hand to Basil. "And thank *you*." The powerful monkey bowed to Basil. "You are a true hero."

Oh, no," Basil replied as his face quickly turned red. "I'm no hero . . . I just . . ."

"That confirms it, dear boy," the professor interrupted with an infectious laugh. "A genuine hero doesn't think of his deeds as being heroic!"

Now it was Basil's turn to change the subject. "No one is going to believe this. Especially my mother back in Maine!"

"Maine?" the caretaker asked. "Where in Maine are you from?"

"Oh, it's just an ordinary place," Basil said with a shrug. "I live in a lighthouse with my mother."

"Not the *Pepperell* Lighthouse?"

"Yes, that's right," Basil said. "You've heard of us?"

"I'm Arthur Pepperell!"

"Great-Uncle *Arthur*? Oh, my mother will *never ever* believe me now!" Basil gave the caretaker a huge hug.

"Maybe in time she will." The caretaker's eyes sparkled. "Who knows what the future may hold— especially in Helios. Basil, you will always be welcome here on Monkey Island. And I may surprise you and your mother with a visit to Maine—once the island is back up to speed, that is."

"Please come." Basil reluctantly pulled away. It was time to go.

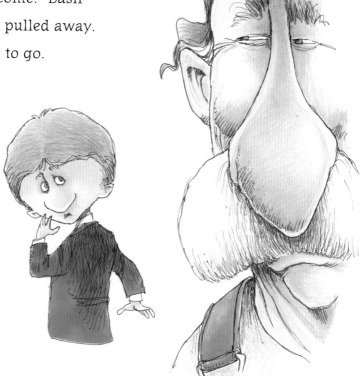

CHAPTER TEN

Taking It Avay

MCGOOKIN LED Basil and Louise back down to the lagoon. As they came closer to the water, Basil looked up and scanned the sky.

"What happened to the owls?" he asked, still jumpy.

"They undoubtedly flew back to Helios, where they were born. Von Röttweil and Vex controlled them with a whistling device that can only be heard by the owls. Once they lost control of the island, they lost control of the owls."

As they neared the submarine, the professor stopped abruptly. A shiny, metal object had popped to the surface of the water. It was covered with prongs. Another one popped up . . . and another.

"Hurry!" The professor scooped up Basil and Louise and staggered away from the water. But before he could say another word, the lagoon erupted with a thunderous explosion. Shock waves sent all three flying.

The professor took the brunt of it as he shielded the children with his body. Basil and Louise sat up in the sand, dazed and disoriented. The submarine was gone.

"Wha . . . what happened, Professor?" Basil's head ached. There was no answer.

"Professor . . . ?" Basil asked again. He tried to clear the ringing in his ears. But the professor was still lying down, his face in the sand. He wasn't moving.

"PROFESSOR!" Louise shrieked. She rushed to his side. It took all their strength to roll the large old man over, but Basil and Louise did it.

Louise began to cry. "He's dead, isn't he?" She put her head on the professor's chest and sobbed. "He was . . . saving us," she began, but then she stopped. "His heart is beating! He's alive!"

The professor coughed as he slowly regained his senses. Rathbone and the caretaker came running, followed by a pack of monkeys. "Quickly," Rathbone said, "get him back inside!"

The monkeys helped the professor up to the safety of the engine room. Basil turned and looked back. *What had caused the explosion?* From the volcano entrance,

he could see past the lagoon and out to sea. Once
again, sunlight reflected off something in the distant
ocean—but this time Basil recognised it. It was the boat
he had sailed back to Maine—Von Röttweil's boat!

By now, a dozen shiny, pronged baubles bobbed
in the water. Soon there were many more, floating
like a school of round, puffed-up blowfish . . . metallic
blowfish.

"Professor!" Basil screamed. *"I know what they are!
They're bombs, and they're drifting towards the island!"*

Everyone gathered and stood in stunned silence. The
island's engines were still shut down. They wouldn't be
repaired for hours.

Out in his ship, watching his fiendish handiwork,
the malevolent doctor stood erect with an air of
boastful victory. His voice was surprisingly loud. "I
gave za island life," he proclaimed, "and now I vill take
it avay . . . to za bottom of za sea!"

The bombs were drifting closer now. *When they strike
the island,* Basil thought, *the bombs will start a chain
reaction of explosions, creating a hole that will sink us all.*

Louise turned to the professor. "What do we do now?"

But the professor didn't have an answer. His mind was still groggy from the explosion in the lagoon. He looked at her sadly. "Perhaps a song, Louise? On your flute, my dear? Make it a good one—your best." He turned to the caretaker. "What do you think, Arthur?"

Louise's soft music began to wind around them. It sounded familiar to Basil, and he began to hum along. Soon all of them were humming.

The caretaker stroked his chin and squinted down at the bombs with anger and disdain. "We mustn't let rage cloud our judgement. And this is no time to give up." Slowly a smile spread across his face. They could all see that an idea had formed, like a sudden move in chess that no one could have foreseen.

"Well," the caretaker said lightly, "since Von Röttweil is determined to sink Monkey Island, maybe we should meet him halfway!"

Everyone stared at him. Then a grin appeared under the professor's bushy moustache.

"Ahhh," the professor said with a knowing look. "I see what you're up to, Arthur! But do you think this barge can withstand the pressure?"

"We'll find out!" The caretaker rushed off to the engine room. "We don't have much choice, do we?"

"What do you want us to do?" For once, Louise was baffled.

"Just come inside and brace yourselves!" By now the caretaker was racing up the scaffolding to a station behind a locked gate. From a massive ring of keys, the caretaker pulled out a tiny brass one and opened the lock at the bottom of the stairs.

He quickly flipped a row of switches. Then he grabbed a thick rope and called to everyone below, "This is it . . . HOLD ON!"

With that, he yanked the rope down.

Crack! Wham! A thunderous whooshing sound followed, like a massive wave hitting the shore. The entire island slanted downwards, sending everything sliding across the floor and crashing into the wall.

"What's going on?" Basil cried.

"He's brilliant!" Louise explained. "The caretaker has opened up all the intake gates on the side of the island facing Von Röttweil and the bombs! When all that water blows out, it's going to create a mountainous wave—pushing the bombs away from the island and right back to Von Röttweil's ship!"

Now it was Von Röttweil who stood in frozen silence, watching as his own bombs were turned against him. Explosions began to rock the sea, safely away from the island. Von Röttweil tried to steer out of harm's way, but bombs kept coming.

Back on the island, the caretaker quickly raised the rope, then pulled another. This released the ballast water on the *other* side of the island, creating a new wave that pushed the bombs even faster towards Von Röttweil.

The monkeys cheered as they watched the doctor panic.

"Good riddance!" Rathbone screeched in anger.

The caretaker gently placed his hand on Rathbone's shoulder. "I understand, old friend, but that's not our way now, is it? If you take on the hatred of your defeated enemy, then what have you won?"

Rathbone looked up at the caretaker. His eyes filled with tears. "You're right. We need to seek justice, not vengeance, if we're going to truly be free."

"And we need to show compassion," the caretaker said. "Even to those we loathe for good reasons."

"But what can be done?" Rathbone turned to watch Von Röttweil. "He sealed his own fate. We're as helpless to save him as he is to save himself."

"Not quite . . ." Louise had that determined look

Basil knew all too well. "Come on, let's go!" She grabbed Basil's hand. Together they ran up the stairs, heading to the top of the volcano.

Meanwhile, Von Röttweil was frantic. The bombs were ripping through the hull, and his ship was sinking. His only hope for escape, the little rowing boat tied to the stern, was already underwater.

Three last bombs were closing in. Von Röttweil leaped off the back of the ship to seek safety in the water. At that moment, all three bombs struck.

Stunned and struggling to stay afloat, Von Röttweil rolled on his back, gasping for air. He lunged at a beam from the hull and reached it before he sank. The nearest land was the island. He had no choice but to kick his way to shore before the frigid waters killed him. And then he saw a sight that made him kick even harder . . . a fin.

The tall, black fin hovered on the surface. Then it was joined by a second fin. As the sharks closed in, the doctor stopped kicking. Only a miracle could save him now, and he did not believe in miracles. He closed his eyes and waited for the end.

That's when he heard an unexpected cry. . . a loud, ear-piercing screech. *Wham!* Something slammed into his back. Terrified, he shut his eyes even tighter.

For a moment, he thought he was dreaming. Instead of bone-crunching jaws, he felt a chilly breeze. Was this the afterlife? When Von Röttweil opened his eyes, the sea was far below. He was sailing through the air, and sharp talons clutched his coat. Beatrice had plucked him out of the water as if he were a big fish.

Looking down at him were Louise and Basil, giggling as they took the defiant doctor back to the island. He kicked and wailed all the way.

CHAPTER ELEVEN

The New World

UPON HIS RETURN to Monkey Island, Von Röttweil was locked up in a cell until he could be transported back to Helios to stand trial.

"All right, young lady," the professor said kindly, "now that Beatrice is back in good health, it's time for you take Basil home. Then you fly directly to Helios. Understand?"

"Yes, sir," she replied with a sheepish grin.

"Good," the professor continued.

"And when you get back to Helios, tell your mother and the rest of the High Council to arrange transport for us along with special security forces for Von Röttweil. I'll be happy to tell her that although you broke the rules again, you've clearly been practising her unification equations on your flute. Good girl. Now say your goodbyes and run along before it gets dark."

"Thanks, Professor. I think I understand about dark energy now. Can we talk about it when I get home?"

"Louise, it would be my pleasure. Maybe you'll share some of your ideas with Basil one of these days. He's going to understand more and more of it, you know."

"That's what my mother told me. He's got a natural countercurrent. That's what happened here on the island, isn't it?"

The professor's eyes twinkled. "It's time for you to head on home, my dear. Stop procrastinating."

Basil was sad to leave Great-Uncle Arthur and his new friends, but he was glad that the monkeys were on their way to becoming self-sufficient. He hugged the caretaker and Rathbone one more time.

"I hope I see you soon, Great-Uncle Arthur," he said in a trembling voice. "I love my mother, but living in a lighthouse in Maine is awfully ordinary."

"I'll be in touch. I promise."

"And you're growing like a weed, Laddie Boy!" the professor added in his booming baritone. "No doubt you'll be one of us soon—or perhaps you already are . . ."

Louise mounted Beatrice and extended her hand to

Basil. As they flew off, they could hear the sound of engines beginning to churn, and smoke appeared from the volcano. The island was once again in motion, safely avoiding detection from the outside world.

"It'll be interesting to come back in a few months to see how they get on, don't you think?" Louise asked. Basil nodded in agreement.

"The island moved quite a distance since we first arrived," she said nonchalantly, "so we're taking a different course back to your lighthouse."

"Really? So why are you telling me that?"

"Well," Louise said in that playful manner that always seemed to lead to adventure, "have you ever seen the six-legged rock toad of the Masivodious Desert? It's on the way . . ."

"No," Basil said with a smile, "but it sounds extraordinary."